Caillou®
And The Rain

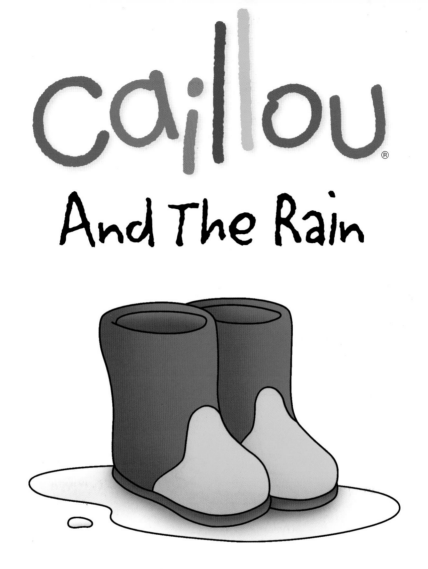

Adaptation of the animated series: Roger Harvey
Illustrations taken from the animated series and adapted by Eric Sévigny

"We have some errands to do, Caillou. And don't forget your boots. It's raining."
"Hooray! I'm going to splash in all the puddles," Caillou said.
First, he put a boot on his left foot.
He looked down at his feet.
"Uh-oh! That feels funny," Caillou thought. Then he realized he had put his boot on the wrong foot.

"Let's put on your raincoat," Mommy said.
"I can do it myself," Caillou replied.
He put his arm in the wrong sleeve and got all tangled up. After several tries, he managed to put it on.
"I did it!" he said proudly.
"Great job, Caillou," Mommy said, handing him his rain hat.

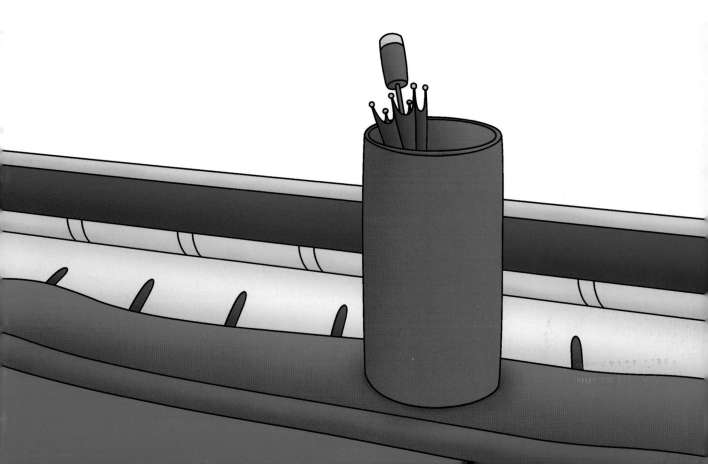

Outside, the rain was coming down very hard. The sight of so much water made Caillou remember something very important. "Mommy..."
"Yes?"
"I have to go to the bathroom," Caillou said.
"Okay, I'll wait for you here." Mommy sighed a little impatiently and put down her umbrella.

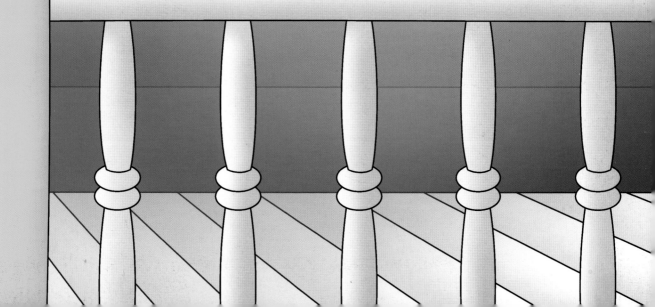

On his way, Caillou almost tripped over a racecar that was in the middle of the carpet. Caillou forgot he had to go to the bathroom and started playing with the car.
"Vroom! Vroom!" Caillou pushed the car and came up against Daddy's feet.
"Caillou," Daddy said.
Caillou looked up.

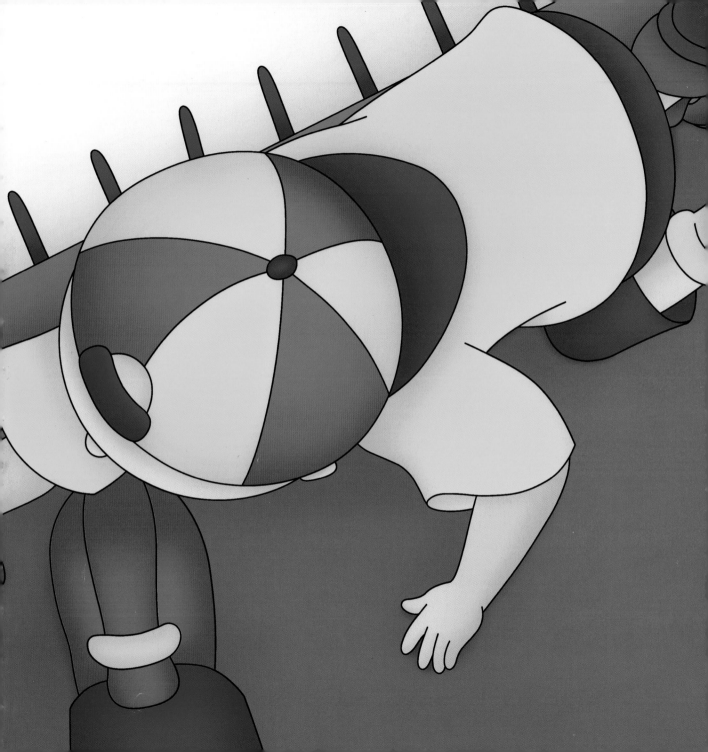

"Yes?" Caillou asked.
"What are you doing here?" Daddy asked.
Caillou looked embarrassed.
"I, uh, had to go to the bathroom," he said.
"Uh-oh, I forgot all about it."
And Caillou dashed into
the bathroom.

While sitting on the toilet, Caillou saw a box
of tissue on top of the toilet tank.
He grabbed the box and started to fly it through
the air like an airplane.
Just then, Daddy opened the door.
"Whee! Look Daddy, a plane!"
said Caillou.

Daddy came closer.
"Your airplane will be here when you get back," he said. "Weren't you supposed to be going out with Mommy?"
Caillou looked at Daddy in alarm.
"Mommy! I forgot!"

Caillou reached the front hall as Mommy was hanging up her raincoat. "Here I am, Mommy! Aren't we going out anymore?" Caillou asked.
"Oh yes, we're still going. But look…" she said and opened the door.
Outside, the sun had come out, but there were still lots of puddles.

Caillou sat down on the floor and put his boots on. On their way out the door, Caillou looked at Mommy in surprise.
"I think you forgot something," he said, pointing to her feet. Mommy realized that she was still in her socks.
"Uh-oh!" she laughed.

They went out onto the porch.
"Yippee! Puddles!" Caillou exclaimed, racing down the stairs. He started splashing happily in the water.
Mommy came up behind him.
"I know it's fun, but we have to do our shopping, Caillou."

Mommy had an idea.

"We can leave our tracks on our way to the store.
Watch." Mommy took a few steps along the sidewalk.
Her feet left footprints on the pavement.

"Your turn now," said Mommy.

Caillou giggled as he followed Mommy, leaving his
footprints all along the sidewalk.

Adaptation of text by Roger Harvey based on the scenario of the CAILLOU animated film series
produced by Cookie Jar Entertainment Inc. (© 1997 CINAR Productions (2004) Inc.,
a subsidiary of Cookie Jar Entertainment Inc.).
All rights reserved.
Original story written by Marie-France Landry.
Illustrations taken from the television series CAILLOU and adapted by Eric Sévigny.
Art Direction: Monique Dupras

The PBS KIDS logo is a registered mark of PBS and is used with permission.

We acknowledge the financial support of the Government of Canada through
the Canada Book Fund for our publishing activities.

Canadian   Patrimoine
Heritage   canadien

We acknowledge the support of the Ministry of Culture and Communications
of Quebec and SODEC for the publication and promotion of this book.
SODEC
Québec

Bibliothèque et Archives nationales du Québec and Library and Archives
Canada cataloguing in publication

Harvey, Roger, 1940-
Caillou and the rain
New ed.
(Clubhouse)
Translation of: Caillou et la pluie.
Originally issued in series: Backpack Collection.
For children aged 3 and up.

ISBN 978-2-89450-870-1

1. Child development - Juvenile literature. 2. Rain and rainfall - Juvenile
literature. I. Sévigny, Éric. II. Title. III. Series: Clubhouse.

HQ781.5.H3713 2012   j305.233   C2011-942120-8

Printed in China
10 9 8 7 6 5 4 3 2 1   CHO1819 JAN2012